LORI DITTMER

GOATS

CREATIVE EDUCATION · CREATIVE PAPERBACKS

Published by Creative Education
and Creative Paperbacks
P.O. Box 227, Mankato, Minnesota 56002
Creative Education and Creative Paperbacks are
imprints of The Creative Company
www.thecreativecompany.us

Design by Ellen Huber
Production by Colin O'Dea
Art direction by Rita Marshall
Printed in the United States of America

Photographs by 123RF (kouziwang), iStockphoto (Altayb, Antagain, brittak, CatuZ, cristianoalessandro, DavidCallan, dimid_86, drakuliren, frahaus, Jamesmcq24, jimkruger, Johny87, JurgaR, LazingBee, lucentius, malerapaso, mihtiander, Pavliha, seakitten, THEPALMER, Linas Toleikis, tomch, vvvita, wonry, wrangle, xalanx), Shutterstock (Inna Astakhova, Eric Isselee, Grigorita Ko, Linas T, Tatyana Vyc, yevgeniy11)

Copyright © 2020 Creative Education, Creative Paperbacks
International copyright reserved in all countries.
No part of this book may be reproduced in any form
without written permission from the publisher.

Library of Congress Cataloging-in-Publication Data
Names: Dittmer, Lori, author.
Title: Goats / Lori Dittmer.
Series: Grow with me.
Includes bibliographical references and index.
Summary: An explanation of the life cycle and life span of goats, using up-close photographs and step-by-step text to follow a goat's growth process from embryo to kid to mature goat.

Identifiers: ISBN 978-1-64026-231-7 (hardcover)
ISBN 978-1-62832-794-6 (pbk)
ISBN 978-1-64000-366-8 (eBook)
This title has been submitted for CIP processing under LCCN 2019938371.

CCSS: RI.3.1, 2, 3, 4, 5, 6, 7, 8; RI.4.1, 2, 3, 4, 5, 7; RF.3.3, 4

First Edition HC 9 8 7 6 5 4 3 2 1
First Edition PBK 9 8 7 6 5 4 3 2 1

TABLE OF CONTENTS

Goats	5
Bearded Ruminants	7
From Embryo to Kid	8
Baby Goats	10
Growing Kids	12
Goat Reproduction	15
Just Browsing	16
Special Stomachs	18
Herd Leadership	21
Dangers	22
Early Goats	25
Goats and Humans	26
Death of a Goat	28
Life Cycle	30
Glossary	31
Websites	32
Read More	32
Index	32

4 — Goats prefer clean, fresh plants to food that is stale or trampled.

Goats are **ruminants**. Like cows and sheep, goats have four stomach chambers. This helps them **digest** food. Male goats are called bucks. Female goats are does.

Domesticated goats live on farms and in backyards all over the world. They are common in Europe, Asia, and Africa. There are hundreds of **breeds**. Goats range in size from the 75-pound (34 kg) pygmy goat to the 300-pound (136 kg) Boer goat.

Goat ears may be small or long and floppy or upright.

BEARDED RUMINANTS

Most goats are white, black, or brown. Sometimes they are a combination of colors. Goat hair can be short or long, silky or coarse. Some goats have horns.

Both males and females may have beards and one or two **wattles**. All goats view the world with rectangular pupils. This helps them see far out to each side.

wattle

FROM EMBRYO TO KID

A goat begins as an **embryo** (*EM-bree-oh*). The embryo grows slowly at first. During the last few weeks before birth, the baby gains most of its weight. It grows hair, too.

The mother goat is pregnant for about 150 days. The process of giving birth is called kidding.

Near kidding time, a pregnant doe might separate herself from the herd.

BABY GOATS

A doe usually has one, two, or three babies at a time. The babies are called kids. Each kid weighs less than 10 pounds (4.5 kg). Despite their small size, kids stand up just minutes after they are born.

The mother goat and her kids soon learn the sound of each other's bleats. Kids climb and butt heads with each other. Until their first birthday, female kids are called doelings. Males are bucklings. Between 12 and 24 months of age, goats are called yearlings.

Young goats butt heads in play; older goats do it to show strength.

Mother goats recognize their kids by sound and smell rather than sight.

11

GROWING KIDS

Kids are born with eight small milk teeth. These teeth are in the lower front gum. At first, kids only drink their mother's milk. Gradually, they begin nibbling hay and grains.

As they grow, goats develop **permanent** teeth. By four years of age, a goat's milk teeth have been replaced. Grinding teeth have grown in the upper and lower jaws. Goats also have a dental pad, a tough ridge with no teeth, on the upper front gum.

Kids drink their mother's milk for about 8 to 10 weeks.

13

Both wild and domestic goats fight to determine their place in the herd.

GOAT REPRODUCTION

Some goat breeds can mate and give birth anytime during the year.

Some female goats are able to reproduce by five months of age. But farmers often wait until the goats are yearlings. Older does have fewer problems during pregnancy and kidding.

The mating season begins when daylight hours grow shorter. During this time, bucks give off a strong odor. They also act aggressively. They charge at other bucks. They might try to butt their owners, too. A buck and doe run and play together. About five months later, their kids are born.

JUST BROWSING

Goats do not eat in grassy fields like cows. They prefer to **browse**. They search out the juicy leaves of bushes and trees. **Agile** goats stand on their hind legs or climb to reach food. Cloven, or split, hooves give them good balance.

Some people think that goats will eat anything, even tin cans. Goats are curious. They might nibble something new as a way of exploring it. But goats are generally picky eaters.

Goats in search of ripe fruits climb argan trees in Morocco.

SPECIAL STOMACHS

Sensitive lips help goats find food that is good to eat.

A goat grabs food with its **prehensile** upper lip and tongue. It chews and swallows. The food moves into the first section of the stomach. It mixes with stomach juices. Then it goes back up to the goat's mouth for more chewing.

After the goat swallows a second time, the food travels through all four stomach chambers. This process can take up to 15 hours. It helps the goat absorb **nutrients** from its meal. Many other animals cannot digest the plants that goats eat.

Goats that live in cold places grow thick, furry undercoats.

Does are usually smaller than bucks of the same breed.

HERD LEADERSHIP

A group of goats is called a herd. It can also be known as a tribe or a trip. Sometimes, goats butt heads. This helps them decide which goat should be in charge of the herd.

Usually, there are two leaders—the female herd queen and the male head buck. The queen takes the best sleeping and eating spots. The head buck is often the biggest and strongest member of the herd. He takes leadership during mating season.

DANGERS

The lead goats keep the other herd members safe. The queen is the first to check out a new plant. She makes sure it is safe to eat. Certain weeds, plants, and mold can make goats sick. Goats can also develop **parasites**.

The head buck and the queen might charge **predators**. Coyotes, wolves, and cougars hunt goats. Sometimes eagles attack kids.

Goats can eat only a small amount of corn, as too much makes them sick.

Cougars often bury their meal and return later to retrieve it.

23

24 — The wild bezoar ibex still lives in mountains from Turkey to Iran.

EARLY GOATS

Goats were among the first animals domesticated by people. Modern goats came from the wild bezoar goat of Asia.

Goats can live happily in many different places. They do not need as much space as cows. Early humans brought goats along as they moved. Goats first came to North America with Spanish explorers in the 1500s.

A person who watches over goats for a living is known as a goatherd.

GOATS AND HUMANS

People raise goats for several reasons. Some goats are kept for their milk. Worldwide, more people drink goats' milk than cows' milk. Goats are also raised for their meat, known as chevon (*SHEH-vuhn*).

Goat breeds such as the Angora have soft, silky hair. This hair is woven into sweaters, blankets, and other goods. Still other people keep smaller goats as pets. Gentle goats are common in petting zoos.

Blankets made from goat hair are soft and warm.

Goat horns are made up largely of keratin, just like human fingernails.

27

DEATH OF A GOAT

The size and condition of a goat's bottom front teeth indicate its age.

28 Goats can live up to 18 years. Some breeds live longer than others. Aging goats die, but their offspring live on. Kids jump, climb, and explore their surroundings. Doelings become does and have kids of their own.

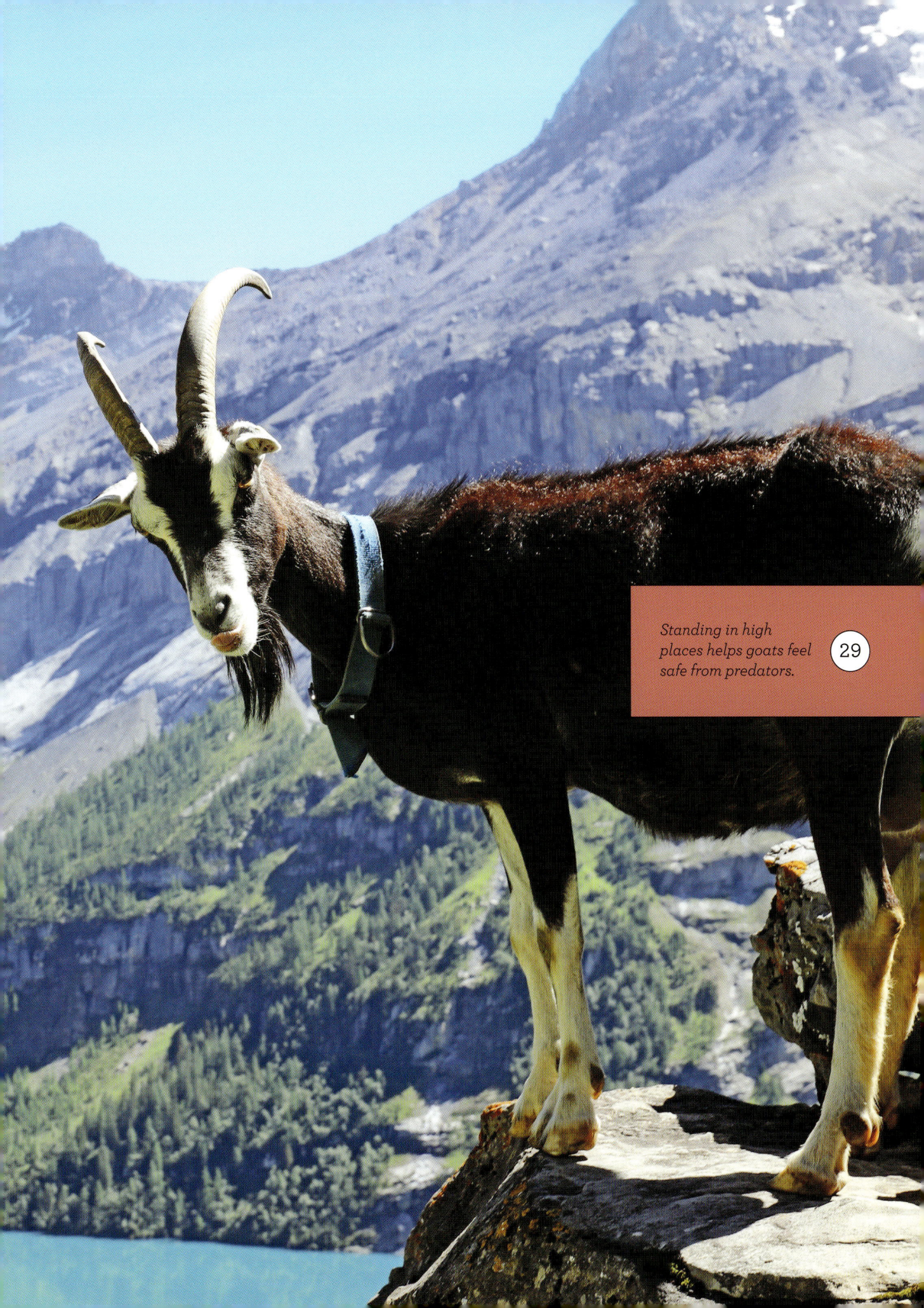

Standing in high places helps goats feel safe from predators.

29

LIFE CYCLE

Embryos grow inside a  mother goat for about 5 months.

 The mother goat gives birth to 1 to 3 kids.

A kid stands up just minutes after birth and drinks its mother's milk.

After a few weeks, the kid  begins to eat solid food.

The kid might gain about 10 pounds (4.5 kg) per month.

By 1 year old, the goat can reproduce.

 The goat is fully grown by 3 years old.

By 4 years old, the goat has 32 permanent teeth.

After 8 to 18 years, the goat dies.

GLOSSARY

agile: *able to move quickly and easily*

breeds: *groups of animals within a species that have similar physical characteristics*

browse: *to feed on high-growing vegetation*

digest: *to turn food into another form*

domesticated: *of an animal kept as a pet or on a farm*

embryo: *an offspring that has not hatched out of an egg or been born yet*

nutrients: *substances needed for growth and to maintain health*

parasites: *organisms that live in or on another organism and take nutrients from it*

permanent: *lasting for a long time*

predators: *animals that kill and eat other animals*

prehensile: *capable of grasping*

ruminants: *warm-blooded animals with hooves and a multi-chambered stomach*

wattles: *fleshy folds of hair-covered skin that hang from the throat*

WEBSITES

DK Find Out: Goats
https://www.dkfindout.com/us/animals-and-nature/domesticated-animals/goats/
Read more about goats and other farm animals

KidZone Animals: Goats
https://www.kidzone.ws/animal-facts/goats/index.htm
Find more goat-related facts, activities, and photos.

Note: Every effort has been made to ensure that the websites listed above are suitable for children, that they have educational value, and that they contain no inappropriate material. However, because of the nature of the Internet, it is impossible to guarantee that these sites will remain active indefinitely or that their contents will not be altered.

READ MORE

Leighton, Christine. *Goats*.
Minneapolis: Bellwether Media, 2018.

Nelson, Robin. *Goats*.
Minneapolis: Lerner, 2009.

INDEX

beards 7
breeds 5, 25, 26, 28
browsing 16, 21, 22
digestion 5, 18
embryos 8, 30
farms 5, 15, 26
food 5, 12, 16, 18, 22, 30
hair 7, 8, 26
herds 21, 22
hooves 16
horns 7

kids 10, 12, 15, 22, 28, 30
life span 28, 30
mating 15, 21
parasites 22
playing 10, 15, 28
predators 22
sounds 10
stomachs 5, 18
teeth 12, 30
wattles 7
yearlings 10, 15